M[illegible] Murders

Abigail Dollar

Crystal Eichlin

Kaitlyn Ferguson

Kaelyn Klaus

Shaelynn McGuinness

ISBN: 9798853653276

Moonlight Murders

CONTENTS

A Lark's Flight

By Kaelyn C. Klaus

Whenever a fairy is born, her birth releases a small amount of dark magic into the world, causing an earthquake or a flood or some other small disaster. The more powerful the fairy, the greater the destruction will be. Too much dark magic will destroy the earth, so it is law that a fairy may give birth only once per year.

Once every thousand moons, an extremely powerful fairy is born. One so powerful the dark magic cannot be contained. It continues to release each moon cycle, for the duration of the fairy's life. The destructive power of this magic grows stronger and more far-reaching with each release, and if allowed to continue, will destroy the earth and all living things. For this reason, these fairies are not allowed to live, and are sought out and killed at birth.

If ever a set of twins were born possessing this dark magic, the world would be thrown into chaos. The birth of two would double the dark magic. Such was the case with Skylark and Meadowlark eight moon cycles ago, and that is why the fairy council took such interest in them.

****

A dainty fairy with silver hair and the most beautiful wings walks toward me, through the tall oaks and maples along the dirt path.

"Hello Grandma Silverlark," I say.

Grandma is giving my sister and me food every other moon.

For a moment she looks angry and triumphant, but I pay no attention to this.

"Hello Skylark," she says, and hands me a small basket.

"What is the fairy council doing now?" I ask, afraid of the answer.

Her eyes shift uneasily as she responds, "I don't know."

I can tell she is lying, but I let it slip by.

"Well, it's time for me to go," I say.

"NO!" Silverlark yells. I start to back away from her; she's never yelled at me before.

"You must stay here, you little pig."

She grabs me by the arm, and reaches for a wand.

"WHO ARE YOU?" I scream.

With a crack of her wand, grandmother is gone. In her place is a tall thin fairy, with dark hair that flows down her back. She has huge, elegant dark purple wings. There is no doubt about it, this is Ensley, a member of the fairy council. She found me.

I struggle to break free of her iron-like grip.

“What’s your name?” Ensley asks.

“Sk…..” I start, But then I realize, she doesn't know who I am.

“Meadowlark,” I say.

“Your grandmother said that Meadowlark doesn’t usually come.”

“Well I did today!” I say.

With a twist, I free myself from Ensley’s grip. I turn and dash toward the hidden cave where Meadowlark and I live. I hope Ensley will be too surprised to come after me. Shouts fill the air as I run. I veer off the path and head deep into a part of the woods I don’t recognize. Hopefully, if I don’t recognize it, neither will Ensley. I run for what feels like hours. Finally, I pause to catch my breath. I look back the way I came, listening for shouts. Silence. I’m hoping that means I wasn’t followed. I also hope that Ensley doesn't know her way around the woods like I do. Looking around though, I realize that while I escaped from one problem, I ran myself into another. I’m completely lost and in unfamiliar territory.

My mind is racing, Why was Ensley disguised as my grandmother? How did she find me?

My grandmother told me that once every thousand moons, an incredibly powerful fairy is born. No one knows why or how this happens. Because this fairy is so powerful, upon her birth, the council seeks her out to kill her. Grandmother said that when the fairy was born, she released more dark magic than just an ordinary fairy. If she were allowed to live, throughout the fairy's life, her dark magic would get stronger, and start to destroy the planet. Since we get our magic from the moon, a fairy can only be killed on a full or new moon. Otherwise the magic release will be so strong, it will cause the planet to explode.

As I ponder this, my mind connects the pieces between the story and my life. Am I the fairy with all the dark magic? My mind is a mess of confusion. If I am that fairy, why wasn't I killed at birth? Is that why my parents hid me, and raised me in secret?

My mind is asking questions and answering them just as quickly.

If I am that fairy, then my sister must be too. We are twins after all.

In all of fairy history, there have never before been twins born with the immense dark magic.

If my magic will keep getting stronger, then I must find a place away from all living things, where my sister and I can live the remainder of our lifetime. First I need to get supplies from our cave. I must find a way back to the path. As I push through the underbrush and shove my way around huge trees, my senses are alert for Ensley. She may be beautiful, but she can be deadly, and she is cunning. Just ahead of me I see the path, and beyond that our cave.

"Meadowlark. Are you there?"

I am eager to tell her about my discovery, and see what she thinks of my plan.

As I make my way toward the cave, I realize something is horribly wrong. The cave has been trashed, and all around me are signs of a fight. Meadowlark is nowhere in sight.

Meadowlark has been taken by the fairy council!

My heart drops so far down that it aches. I must find Meadowlark. If I don't, the council will kill her.

"Meadowlark!" I cry out in pain.

I sink to the ground, my heart too heavy to move. I know this is not the time to get lost in my grief; I need to find my sister, but I don't know if I can get up. The pain of all the what if's is just too great.

With exasperating slowness my blue-green wings start to flap. I lift off the ground and begin to gain altitude. I scan the ground below and the sky ahead of me, looking to see if I can spot the council. Far in the distance, I see the silhouettes of a group of fairies flying towards a high mountain range. My energy starts to drain, and my feet once again touch the ground. Fairies my age can't fly for very long. We have frail wings that can support our body only for a short time. Flying for any longer than an hour depletes too much of our energy. The older a fairy gets, the longer she can fly.

I run to our cave to gather food and my dagger, as well as my mirror of visions. This allows me to see small glimpses of the future. I look around the cave one last time, and start off to rescue my sister.

Heading west towards the silhouettes, the scenery is a blur of greens, browns and grays all mixing together. I'm deep in thought, and the time goes by quickly. It was noon when I left, and I suddenly realize the sun is about to set. Reaching the base of the first mountain, I decide to set up camp. I'm thinking about rescuing Meadowlark, and as I drift off to sleep, I wonder if isolating ourselves will be enough to stop our magic from destroying the world.

I wake to the sounds of birds chirping. The sun is warm and the air is sweet, but I hardly notice. I don't waste any time, and start my climb up the first mountain. I know that the council will be taking Meadowlark to the temple in the valley on the other side of the mountains, where they will perform the sacrifice. The mountains are large, but with the fast pace I set for myself, it doesn't take long for me to cross several of them. Looking back, I marvel at my progress.

Nightfall comes, and I settle down with my mirror of visions. The mirror starts to glow. It shows me a picture of my sister. She is tied and being drug along the ground. Her arms and legs are raw and bleeding, and her eyes are lifeless. I see the quick rise and fall of her chest, and sigh with relief. She's alive!

"Meadowlark!" I cry.

I have never seen my twin look so helpless. If I don't rescue her, it will be my fault if she is killed. I slip the mirror away, not wanting to see any more. Will I make it in time? I fall asleep wondering how I will live with myself if I don't.

Morning comes, and I flutter into the air to see where my sister is. I don't see anyone, but I do see the temple. I am almost there! As I land, I wonder if it would be faster to fly. I'd have to fly in short bursts, but it would be faster than walking. I lift back into the sky, and head for the temple.

Soon I realize that it is farther away than I thought. It will take me several days to reach it, even if I fly. Last night's moon was a waxing gibbous. I only have a few more days until the full moon. The day of sacrifice. Instead of resting after my flight, I resume climbing the mountain on foot. It is slower than flying, but better than resting, and it feels good to be getting closer.

I have alternated walking and flying nonstop for the whole day, and I am nearly dead with fatigue, but I refuse to stop. Thoughts of my sister propel my weary body forward, and I continue to travel through half the night, before finally succumbing to exhaustion. I'm asleep almost instantly.

In the light of the new day, I see the temple and the council. At least I think it's the council. I'm still too far away to tell for sure. If I travel all day today, and again through the night, by tomorrow I should be within an hour's flight of the temple.

I'm not sure if I want another glimpse of the future, but I can't resist pulling out my mirror again. This time, instead of seeing my sister, I see the whole world. As I watch, it starts to crack and fall apart. In the very center, I see myself and a faint silhouette of my sister. The meaning smacks me hard in the face. If we don't find someplace far away from people, I will destroy the world. The mirror is showing me that we both have incredibly powerful dark magic, but mine is even more immense than Meadowlarks. I wonder again if isolation is the answer. What if it's not enough?

The light from a nearly full moon guides me as I continue walking and flying into the night. I am so tired that I can't go on. Tomorrow is the day of the full moon. If all goes well, I will arrive at the temple, and rescue my sister. I collapse on the ground, neither my wings nor my legs able to keep me upright any longer. I am too tired for the mirror of visions, and fall asleep the instant my eyes close.

I awake before dawn and climb that last bit to the temple. Members of the fairy council are asleep all around the temple. I see Moonshadow, Atum, Jasmine, Flin, Bloom, and Ensley. Tied far away from the council, somewhat behind the temple, is Meadowlark. She is battered and bruised, but still alive. I nearly faint with relief. I am too tired to mount a rescue now, so I decide to rest until sun up. I'm only going to get one chance at this. I don't want to mess it up.

Feeling the sun's warmth on my face, I open my eyes to rose pink clouds as the sun peaks above the horizon. Not wasting any time, I dash to where my sister is tied. Her eyes are open, but unseeing. She is barely alive.

"Meadowlark, it's me, Skylark." I whisper.

"Skylark?" It's barely audible.

Tears well in my eyes."How could they do this to you?"

She wets her lips and tries to speak. "They think I'm you."

"That's my fault!" I sob. "Ensley was disguised as grandmother, and I told her that I was you."

She looks confused."But Ensley is here."

"I guess she decided that I was you."

She nods. "I knew you would find me."

I smile sadly at her. "You've always been there for me. It's the least I could do."

Something occurs to me suddenly, why did they almost kill her? Wouldn't they want her alive, if they are going to sacrifice her? Unless... is she bait in an even bigger plan? Are they trying to weaken me?

"Oh no. Oh no no no no," I say.

"Why hello, Skylark. Glad you finally made it," says a very familiar voice.

Ensley's eyes are dark pools of anger. I thought she was a good person, just trying to protect the fairies, but now I'm not so sure.

"If you knew Meadowlark was not me, why did you nearly kill her?"

"I know you have the mirror of visions, and I knew when you saw your sister like this, you would be weak and helpless, and we could capture you more easily," Ensley says.

Ensley is right, I hate that the sight of a bleeding Meadowlark makes me helpless, but it does. It's just fairy nature.

"So you need to kill me?" I ask. "But why do you have to make a sacrifice?" I wonder before she can answer my first question. "I see it now. You are power hungry," I answer my own question. "and you think that sacrificing me to the moon will not only save the fairies, it will make you more powerful too," I say.

"Silence! Your ignorance is a disgrace. You know nothing about the power we will gain."

"So you will gain power somehow," I say.

"Yes, in sacrificing the fairy born with too much dark magic, all those present will receive the thanks of the moon. That is what we have been doing for many years. We have been alive since the beginning. The moon gives us youth, and makes us stronger. It also controls the fairies' minds, ensuring our rule forever," Ensley says. "You two are twins, so we will use you both, and gain more power than ever before!"

"So Meadowlark does have power; I suspected

as much."

Throughout this conversation, I have been working at the bonds restraining my sister. I have almost untied her. In a sudden blur of movement, Ensley grabs me, and pulls me away from Meadowlark.

"Let me go!" I scream. "I need to save my sister!"

"Oh no you don't," Ensley says. "What you need to do is die."

Die. The word catches my attention. Ensley can't keep the world in the dark about this crazy moon magic stuff anymore. She needs to be stopped. A sad thought occurs to me.

Meadowlark probably won't survive, not after what the council has put her through. They will sacrifice her because we both have the dark magic in our blood.

With this realization, I fight harder against Ensley. I need to kill my sister myself before the council sacrifices her. I break free from Ensley, and run back to Meadowlark's side.

"Meadowlark," I say as fast as I can. "The council won't let you live. They will sacrifice you, just like they want to sacrifice me. Then they will use the power they gain from the moon for their own selfishness and greed."

She frowns, and then her eyes widen. I reach into my bag and grab the dagger. Its sharp blade gleams silver blue.

"Skylark, you can't possibly mean this!" Meadowlark cries.

I look into her beautiful green eyes, and she knows I do. "I understand," she says. "Go well my sister. Stop the council." Then she closes her eyes.

"You read my mind," I say with a sad smile.

My hand trembles. This is the worst thing I have ever done. I raise my hand, and plunge the dagger into my sister's heart. To save her, and the rest of the world.

"No!!!" someone screams. Maybe it's me. I look up. Ensley is standing perfectly still, and is as cold as ice.

"We needed her. For the sacrifice."

"Well," I shout with tears streaming down my face,"then I'll do the same to you, and you can join her in the sky!"

Anger bubbles up inside me. Ensley lied to the fairies. All this time she pretended to save us, when instead, she and the council stole the power of the moon. This will continue unless I stop her. I have to be the one. No one else knows about this.

My eyes start to glow, and filled with not only my dark magic and rage, but my sister's too, I charge towards Ensley. The tip of my dagger pierces her heart. She falls to the ground, and I stab her again and again.

I won't be able to live. I think. Not after killing my own sister. My own dear sister, who used to insist that brussel sprouts were the best food in the world. I let out an animalistic wail of anger and grief.

Now I know what the mirror meant. That second vision. I don't have to isolate myself. I have to kill myself.

I don't understand why I don't seem to have to mentally prepare for this. I just now came to this conclusion, and I'm ok with it I don't like it, but I know it needs to be done.

Then I wonder for a moment if killing Enley was

the right thing to do. She killed children born with dark magic. It's an awful and gruesome thing, but did she have a choice? Furthermore, did she need to take the power from the moon, and use it to live forever? I wonder vaguely what will happen in the future. With the council gone, what will happen to the next child born with dark magic? Maybe what I am about to do will change the old ways for years to come. I hope so, I know Meadowlark would hope so too.

I close my eyes, and start to fly up towards the heavens. My gold hair streams out behind me, as I use my magic to save the world from our dark power. I reach out with my mind, and close the cracks in the world. I make the oceans and rivers fill with clean water instead of muddy and poisoned water, and I rid the world of the council's way of ruling. I send my story into the minds of all of the fairies. I let them know what their rulers have been doing.

I open up a crack underneath the rest of the council, and I bury them alive. I don't feel any regret, just power. Power and rage so much rage.

Then I raise the dagger dripping with my sisters and Ensley's blood, and bury it in my own chest. I feel my body falling at the same time as I feel my spirit rising. I know that I will join my sister, and we will be together now, without any more sadness or loss. I smile and close my eyes, letting the earth open one more time to let my body Rest In Peace.

****

It's a still night, and the full moon shimmers softly on the grass. In a meadow are two small graves. Not far away is a temple. A statue stands at the head of each grave. One is a fairy with long dark hair and purple wings; the other is a fairy with long golden hair and blue-green wings.

A silvery spirit drifts down to hover before the graves. Slowly, she steps forward and touches the cheek of the statue of the fairy with purple wings.

“Meadowlark,” the spirit whispers. “I am sorry.”

The End

That person is you

That Person is You

By Crystal Eichlin

The Start:

A guard passes by a jail cell with someone standing inside it. That someone looks familiar. Although it may not seem like you might know that person, they still oddly…stand out to you.

That person is you.

Just kidding! That person is actually not you! And yes, I am breaking the fourth wall right now! It's only for the moment though, as soon as the story continues, I'm back to being my clueless self and not knowing that practically a lot of people are reading my "tragic" story right now. That's the routine for making stories normally. Anyway, let's actually get to the story! Sorry for the interruption.

While I'm waiting for a taxi, it finally arrives. I am getting a ride because I get too paranoid walking alone at night, plus the rain will get me soaking wet. I went inside the car and I shut the car door, and watched the rain pour down my window while the car started to drive. Ah, the rain is so beautiful, especially at night. When the moon shines across the pavement. The moment it shines on the buildings, while raindrops fall from the sky, it's something so unique and special.

I'm patiently sitting silently in the vehicle, I start wondering what the time might be since I've recently lost my only watch that I had, and I don't want to be late again to my mother's house. I lean in to talk to the taxi driver to ask what the time is. "Excuse me sir, do you know what time it is? I've recently lost my only watch I had, so it would be a huge help."

The taxi driver glanced at the time and looked back at me, "It's currently 9:00. Now that I think about it, I need to arrive at my daughter's sixth birthday before she goes to sleep. Ah jeez. I know I decided to pick up one more person so I could get more money to help with my family but I really need to get home."

Honestly, after hearing that I started feeling bad. Suddenly words start spilling out of my mouth, "Sir, I'm sorry I don't really need a ride I just get afraid when it gets dark. You can just drop me off here! My house actually isn't too far away. No need to keep you from your family for too long!" I smile.

The man looks at me through his rearview mirror and begins to speak. "Really? You're actually serious?"

I tilt my head, "Why of course! How silly for you to ask that question!"

He starts to form a humongous grin, "Thanks good sir! You can take my umbrella when you walk out so it doesn't pour on you, it's the least I could do!"

I laugh a little, "Thank you very much. I'll really need it out there! I really appreciate it." The man stops driving and goes into parking mode. I open the car door and walk out and I shut the door behind me. I then walk to the other car door in the front and open it and grab the umbrella, "You sure you won't be needing this when you get out of your car?"

He looks at me with absolute no worry within his face, "Yeah, I won't need it. I can survive a little rain! It's not like it's gonna bite." I look at him and laugh one last time, "Alright! Have a nice night." Before I leave he asks me one more thing, "By the way- what's your name?"

I look at him and give a little smile, "It's Eliaz." I then shut the door and I turn around and start walking away from the car and then it proceeds to drive off into the distance.

I have arrived at my mother's house. I open the front door and I walk in, it seems like my mother has already fallen asleep so I probably should be quiet enough to not wake her up. I go into the kitchen and I grab a small snack to eat and I drink some cold water to quench my thirst before I head to bed.

I open the door that proceeds into my room. I look around to see if anything is not how it was before just in-case. I look around the room and I start walking towards my bed and I look inside my dresser. I find the pajamas that I'm going to wear to bed. I turn around and I look into the nightstand drawer to double check to see if my safety knife is still there. I close the drawer after seeing that it is present and I start changing into my clothes.

After I'm done changing, I walk out of my room and do my normal nightly routine, after some time I walk back into my room and head towards my bed. I push over the covers and I slip into bed.

I grab my TV remote that's on my nightstand and I turn the TV on. I flip the channels over and over until I finally find something that could possibly help me fall asleep. Having the TV off gets me really nervous and sketched out. It would be too dark for me to see around the room and focus on if anyone is in it with me. As soon as I found something I liked, I proceeded to place the remote back on the nightstand and I'd turn over and close my eyes.

I'm peacefully asleep, and my alarm begins to start ringing like crazy! The annoying noise wakes me up straight away and I slam my alarm to turn it off. I sit up and I look around my room and I let out a good ol' yawn. I instantly realize that I'm already five minutes late to get ready for school and I quickly hop out of my bed to go change into my clothes that I'm going to be wearing to school today.

After I change my clothes I instantly proceed to do my normal daily routine, I quickly run over to the front door so I can exit the house and get to school before it is too late.

"Eliaz! Aren't you going to eat breakfast? It's bad to go to school hungry y'know!" I yell out to her

"Sorry mom I can't! I got to go before the bus leaves! Love you!" I open the front door and quickly rush out of the house and the door slams shut.

I run straight to the bus stop, and the bus arrives just in time. I wait for the bus doors to open and I run up the bus stairs. I walk inside the bus to find a seat, once I see one open I instantly sit down. I usually sit by myself because sitting by someone makes me super nervous. I don't trust a lot of people, mostly because of my paranoia. I calmly let out a sigh and look out the window.

After some time of driving on the bus, we finally arrived at our destination! The bus doors open for everyone to get out, and I stand in line waiting for everyone to get off the bus. I really hope we get off the bus more quickly from now on. I hate being in a single file line where someone is behind you and you never know what they're gonna do because you don't have eyes on the back of your head. Once I'm out of the bus the doors immediately close, after everyone's off, and the school bus drives away. Looks like it's the start of a new day today!

I walk around the front of the school talking to a few friends before I decide to head to first period. After I'm done speaking with everyone, and wishing them a good-morning, I open the door and walk inside the school.

After a while, I finally open the door to the first period and as I walk in, the bell instantly rings. Thank god I got here in time before it did! Otherwise I could've been considered tardy. I look for my usual seat in the back. I sit down and look into my backpack for the usual supplies that we need to start class.

I get out the workbook that we need for this period and I begin to read it, but I instantly get distracted and start toying with my pencil.

A student walks into our classroom, I stop doing whatever I was doing with my pencil and I look up at the front of the classroom. Something seems a little off about him, it's hard to explain. I just have a certain feeling when I just.. look at him. I find it kind of strange that he changed schools towards the end of the school year, and towards graduation. Maybe I should try and get to know him? It's just like me to introduce myself to every new person!

The teacher begins to speak. "Everyone, listen up. We have a new student. Why don't you introduce yourself to the class?" I look at the new kid with intent, he seems very interesting to me for some reason.. The student becomes pretty silent, so the teacher speaks again. "Hello? Did you not hear me? I said to please introduce yourself. It's rude to ignore your teacher, you know. Not a very good impression either." The new kid finally begins to speak but he seems really annoyed.

"My name is Asahi, I'm 17 and I'm new here. I have nothing else to say. It's a waste of time talking to these people if they aren't even listening, literally what is the point in this? Can I just go sit down in my seat and get to work? I'm not really interested in this whole introducing thing. It's extremely boring."

I tilt my head while staring at the new kid, he seems kinda serious! Very mature, too. I wonder what his personality is like. Maybe I should try talking to him after class? Hopefully I don't sound too weird though, that'd be bad. I would definitely not want to upset a guy like him.

The teacher lets out a sigh and nods, he then

points at where Asahi's seat is. Coincidentally, it seems that Asahi sits right next to me. I really do hope we get along otherwise it's gonna be true hell when I have to be seated next to him every single day. I could probably ask for a seat change though, if the teacher would let me.

After Asahi sits down and after a lot of thinking the class begins to start. I try my best to pay attention in class for the time being, but I keep glancing over at Asahi, it seems like he is almost going to fall asleep? Honestly, just watching him makes me want to fall asleep too, so I end up letting out a yawn and then I go back to trying to pay attention to the teacher.

After about an hour the class finally ends. Everyone begins to leave the classroom. I get up from my seat and I grab my backpack. Then I see Asahi about to leave the classroom and I quickly rush over to him and I grab his wrist. He instantly looks at me with, of course, an annoyed look on his face.

I let go of his wrist and I began to speak to him with a shaky voice, honestly that face makes me quite afraid of him "I apologize, Asahi. My name is Eliaz. May I talk to you for the remaining passing period? I'd like to get to know you better, if that's alright with you."

Asahi stares at me for thirty seconds intensely, it's very intimidating. He then lets out a sigh, "Fine. I'm actually quite surprised that you managed to remember my name. We can walk around the school together for passing periods and we can talk during it and at lunch. Just don't be annoying."

I look at Asahi with a confused expression, "Well of course I remembered your name, it's not that hard to remember a person's name that they just said not too long ago! Anyways, I'm very excited to know more about you!"

Asahi looks at me with deadly eyes, "You already sound annoying. I'm starting to regret my decision. Oh well, let's just start heading out now." After Asahi is finished speaking we proceed to head out of the classroom and begin getting to know each other. While we walked to many sorts of places during school, when on our breaks, and after school, I saw some sort of shady man trying to get our attention. I quickly speed-walked away with Asahi to our houses because we live pretty close to each other. I just ended up shrugging it off though, not important right?

Until it was. After a couple months of being best friends with Asahi, every single day of those months I always saw that person. They were always trying to get our attention but I always ran away with Asahi whenever he showed up because it was really creepy. A couple times I tried talking to Asahi about it, but he didn't think it would be something to make a big deal out of. I started becoming more paranoid by each passing day.

One day, I was at this private place with Asahi. We were just hanging out like we usually do, and he was just judging the hell out of me like he always does. Suddenly I realize someone is behind him, slowly edging towards him. My eyes widen in shock, and I yell at him to move out of the way but he looks at me with concern and he doesn't move at all. I yell at him again, "ASAHI! YOU NEED TO MOVE NOW!"

The person then turns out to be right behind Asahi, he looks like he's wearing a hood. I push

Asahi out of the way just in time before the person makes a move. The unknown person then stares at me. Before I get to see what he's holding, I reach out for something in my jacket, very slowly so the man does not notice.

Asahi carefully watches this in shock, not moving a muscle. The man tries to take out something that he's holding. Before I look and see what the man is holding I look at Asahi and yell at him once more, but Asahi has no reaction to it. I pulled a knife out of my jacket quickly. Before I left with Asahi to hang out, I brought my safety knife just in case the man was going to follow us again. I wasn't about to take any chances on it.

The man drops the thing that he is holding and he tries to take the knife away from me, while also saying a bunch of words that I cannot seem to hear because of how afraid I was. Suddenly out of nowhere, I stab him right in the chest because of how afraid I am. Blood starts dripping off the knife onto the floor, and I've now just realized what I have just done.

The man collapses on the floor and while he falls the hood reveals his identity. The man that I had just stabbed was the taxi driver that wanted to be with his family that one rainy night. I start shaking and sweat pours down my face. I look at Asahi, who is staring at me.

I realize that the taxi driver dropped a gift, I bend down over his body and I pick up the gift that is beside him. It says that it's addressed to "Eliaz" which is clearly my name. I open the gift and it's an extremely expensive watch. I assume that the taxi driver got me this watch because of how I lost my old one. The new watch came with a note saying how grateful he was that I let him go spend time with his family. I immediately start feeling horrible and I turn to Asahi.

I start trembling and stumbling towards him and I try to speak, "Asahi, this is my taxi driver.. It seems like the whole time he was just trying to repay me for what I did. I didn't- I didn't mean to kill him." Asahi then looks at me in utter disbelief. "Eliaz, what have you done?" The exact words I kept repeating in my head too. "You KNOW you're going to be arrested? You should've just let him make the first move. You could've- you could've asked what he wanted with us. Why did you even bring a knife in the first place? How are you going to take care of this?"

I begin panicking and I decide to tell him the hardest thing that I've ever had to say in my life. "Asahi, get out of here. I'm going to call the police on myself. I shouldn't have done this to him when I could've just asked what he wanted. I can't just cover this up- I can't just run away from this. I need to face my own problems for once. Please, just go."

Asahi then looks angry at me, "I'm not just going to leave you like this. Why are you this ignorant? I can't leave you. The one that should run away is you, not me. I should take the blame. You get out of here. Alright?" I notice something. He's not afraid of me, he's afraid for me. Before I can even respond, he takes out the knife that was in the person's body so that the only fingerprints that are on the knife are his.

I start yelling at him, and slurring my words. He doesn't listen to a word I'm saying, he takes out his phone and calls 911. After he's finished speaking on the phone he hangs up and puts it back in his pocket and turns to me. He gives me a sincere look, like he doesn't regret it at all.

I look at him with hope that he might change his mind, and I start speaking. "Why, Asahi. Don't you understand what I did was wrong? You shouldn't take the blame for me. I just murdered someone, it's not like this is some casual robbery. I actually killed someone.. You know that even if you do try and frame yourself for this they're just gonna end up finding out right? What's the point?"

He looks at me and smiles, "Of course I know that, Eliaz. You're my best friend, even though you're the most annoying person I've ever met- that doesn't change a thing. There shouldn't be a point to why I want to take the blame." I start to notice police cars coming with sirens, and the lights that are flashing blue and red. I begin to say something, but before I could, he says "Run, you idiot."

I become so angry with myself, and him. I begin running away, farther and farther as fast as I could. I stop and look behind me, I watch Asahi get arrested and handcuffed. I can't help but start feeling inconsolable, tears start swelling up in my eyes. I softly start to say one last thing before I go. "Goodbye." I turn around, and walk away.

The End.

Fireflies

By Abigail Dollar

For as long as I can remember, I've dreamt of being a knight. When I was younger, my mom read me stories of the brave knights slaying fire-breathing dragons, fighting off ferocious beasts, and being a hero. Sadly, she had fallen ill when I was five. Soon after she was diagnosed, she died.

About a year after my mom died, my dad married a widow named Athena, whose husband had been murdered under very suspicious circumstances. She wasn't as kind as my dad said she was. when my father went out to work on the farm or go to the market she was a cruel, strict, old witch.

She would yell at me for walking too loud or if I slouched. Around my dad she acted like she cared, but when he turned his back she would give me devilish glares and boss me around. When I decided to tell my dad that I wanted to be a knight, Athena said that I would never survive, she told me that I was too skinny and weak.

So I decided to work and work for seven years. When I would help my father on the farm, I would move the hay and milk buckets. I would practice my sword techniques with sticks. I would do as much as I could to prepare for becoming a knight.

The morning of the knighting ceremony, I had woken up and walked down the hallway into the kitchen, she had made my dad and me breakfast.

"So, dad, I have my knight ceremony today," I said, pushing my eggs around on my plate.

"I'll try to make it, but I work today," he responded. "But you have fun, ok?"

"I'll try," I responded when he finally looked at me.

"I won't be able to make it, I have plans for today, but you should definitely go, just be home for dinner." Athena said abruptly.

"I was planning on it." I snapped back. I stood up and put my plate in the sink.

When I arrived, I realized that I was the youngest person there.I stood at the gates to the king's knighting ceremony. I could hear my heart pounding in my ears. I walked through the doors of the arena, the scent of popcorn and funnel cake flooded my nose. There were hundreds of voices echoing throughout the arena, waiting for the event to begin.

"Hear-ye hear-ye, the trials are about to begin!" The king's assistant yelled out to the crowd. I make my way to the entrance table, an older man with brunette hair, with grey streaks in it turns around and looks down at me with a confused look.

"Hey lil' buddy, shouldn' ya be in the crowd?" He asks me, lifting an eyebrow.

"No, I'm here for the same reason as you," I answered him with a slight smile.

"This is fur' grown men, not weak little boys. You must be confused. How old are ya, like six?" The man smirked.

"No, I'm 16 and I bet I've been training for this for longer than you."

"Ha! Shur' ya have buddy boy! I've been training fur' this fur' four years!" He stood up all of the way, trying to look more powerful. "Beat that!" He yelled along with a laugh.

"Seven," I said, watching as his face dropped. Suddenly music started playing as the first man was called up.

"Gregory Smith" the announcer called as a Small man walked into the arena. We all watched as the bars were lifted away from the opening of the dark cave-like hole in the wall and a medium-sized, black dragon with gold-tipped wings and horns stepped out. The crowd gasped, as the man tried to back out but the guards had closed the gate. So the little man attempted to fight the dragon, but without even one hit he was burnt to a crisp on the spot.

The men slowly started to pour out if they weren't one of the few who succeeded, they died.

"Elliot Green!"

Finally! I thought. I had just stepped onto the

field when it hit me, the feeling of fireflies in my stomach. Am I nervous!? I thought No! I have been training for this for half of my life! I can't stop now. The sweat dripped down my face as I drew my sword and was ready to fight. They released the dragon. I took a deep breath, and ran as fast as I could at the dragon, swung my sword, hitting it. The crowd went crazy. I tried to pull my sword out, but it was no use. I climbed up the side of the dragon using my sword. I pulled as hard as I could on my sword from the top, and almost fell off when I finally got it out. I held on with all of my strength as it swung me around like a little rag doll. Finally, I got a chance and I stabbed it in the back. The dragon let out a loud screech, as It threw me off and into the wall, I hit the ground with a loud thud. Oww. I groaned as I stood up and wiped what was either blood or sweat off of my face.Everyone was cheering for me as I walked over to the dragon, it had already fallen to the ground, so I lifted my sword high above my head and stabbed the dragon in the head.

I fell to the ground and clutched my side with my hand. I definitely broke at least one rib. I looked up to see the king nodding his head. As I made my way up to the stands with everyone else, I heard a familiar voice behind me. I turned my head to see a kid from my class sitting right behind me with a grin on his face.

"You put on quite a show, Green. Too bad the King is never gonna pick someone as scrawny and short as you!" He looked rather formal for an event like this: a fancy green suit and black tie, complementing his jet black hair.

"It's not like you could know much more about

the King than me." I said knowing I was probably wrong.

"Well, I-"

"The King has made his decision!" The announcer said over the crowd's chatter.

"James Conner, Preston Sphinx, Carter Westbrook, and Elliot Green. Please make your way to the castle."

As we were walking to the castle, I noticed that there was another young man who had Made it. He looked to be about 18 with dirty blonde hair and green eyes, wearing armor that was at least three sizes too big for him. He must have noticed me staring because he looked over at me and smiled.

" It was my dads armor, my mom insisted I wore it," he said. " My name's Preston, Preston Sphinx," he said, sticking his hand out.

"I'm Elliot Green," I responded, shaking his hand, and smiling back.

When we arrived at the castle, the king's assistant was waiting for us at the gate.

"Follow me please." He said, as he started to walk into the gates. The court yard was full of people yelling and congratulating us. The king's assistant led us into the castle. As the doors shut behind us, the noise from the people outside stopped, but I could tell that it was still there.

The king was waiting for us at his throne, his assistant bowed and we all followed in his lead.

"Thank you for competing in our competition," he said, his assistant handed each of us metals with little dragons on them. "You're all very brave and I can tell that you will do great. Training starts on Monday, I can go home now, it's my dinner time."

We walked out of the castle and through the

crowd of people. I continued on the road and into the country, when I noticed that someone was behind me. I turned around to see Preston.

"Hi," he said, running to catch up with me.

" Hey, do you live over here too?" I asked.

" Yeah, me and my mom live on Olive street. What about you?"

" My dad, my step mom and I live on Barkley avenue." I responded, I had no clue anyone my age lived near me.

"Welp. Here's me, wanna hang out tomorrow?" he said as he walked away down a little street.

"Sure! Bye!" I said as I waved at him. I don't have many friends so it's nice to have someone I know so close to me.

When I Arrived at home, I noticed that the door was wide open. I walked in and tried to close it, but I realized that the hinges were broken. I picked up the screw that was on the ground and tried to put it back in the hole but it wouldn't go in. I turned around and continued into the kitchen, where Athena was pulling something out of the oven.

"Hello Elliot," she said as she smiled, holding a pan of fresh baked cookies.

"Hi," I replied as I sat at the counter.

She puts the cookies on a plate, and sets the plate in front of me. "Have a cookie, they just came out of the oven." Her smile grows wider,

"Thank you." I say, grabbing a cookie and slipping out of the chair. "Where is dad?" I ask. "He's usually home by now." I said worryingly, because he's never late.

"I think he's working late," she said as she walked over to the sink.

"Do you know when he will be home?"

"I'm not quite sure, dear, how did your knight thing go?" She grabbed her cup of tea and walked over to the counter, where she had set the cookies.

"It was fine, I made it in," I said, leaning against the door frame.

" Good job!" She said and smiled.

"Ok, well I'm gonna go to my room." I said as I walked to my room. I closed the door behind me and sat on my bed and stared out my window. I lay back, my feet hanging off the end of my bed, and I closed my eyes.

I was startled awake by the sound of the tea kettle screeching. I look at the clock on the wall. 12:30. I must have fallen asleep, I thought to myself. I pushed myself up and off of my bed, a shiver ran down my spine as my feet hit the cold floor. I walked over to my door and pushed it open, it was silent. I ran into the living room and looked out of the window, the only car in the driveway was the old rusty orange farm truck that my dad usually drove. I wandered the house looking for any sign of my dad, stopping at the glass door in the kitchen that leads out to the corn field. The stocks swayed in the Saturday breeze.

I walked back to my bedroom and grabbed my bag, and started towards Preston's house. I walked along the side of the gravel road, kicking rocks, I could hear sirens in the distance. I look up to a police car and an ambulance barreling past me. They stop at a crowd of people standing on the side of the road crowding around something in the ditch. I break into a run, ducking below peoples arms and pushing my way through the crowd to see what it was. That's when I saw him, my dads lifeless body in the ditch, covered in mud and hay. The murmurs of the people that surrounded me grew quiet and everything went black.

I woke up in a hospital bed attached to a bunch of machines. I turned my head to see Athena in a chair next to me reading a magazine. I looked over at the door as the doctor walked in, I sat up and stared at my lap.

"Oh, you're awake," the doctor said, handing Athena a piece of paper.

"What happened?" I asked.

"You passed out"

Suddenly the memory comes flooding back to me; the images flashing through my head like a kaleidoscope. That's when it hit me. He was dead, but how did he die? I looked at Athena, she had been making excuses for why he hadn't been home recently. Suddenly I felt the fireflies. "What did you do?" I asked, watching the smile fade from her face.

"W-what do you mean dear?" she replied, straightening her posture, I noticed that she normally did that when she was lying.

"What did you do to my father? I know you're the reason why he is dead!" I yelled. Her usually pink cheeks turned a pale white.

"What? I don't understand what you are talking about! I didn't do anything to my husband." She yelled back and reached for the handle of the door. "It is very rude for you to assume that! I'm gonna get the nurse, I don't feel safe with you in here alone!" She reached for the handle of the door, when the nurse came in.

"Eliot Green?" The nurse asked.

"Yes," Athena replied.

"Your all good, your free to go" The nurse replied

We walked out of the hospital.

“ Get in the car.” She said when I stopped at the door.

“No, I know you did something to my dad and I’m gonna prove it!”

“Get in now!” She was yelling now, and it was drawing a lot of attention from the people in the parking lot.

“No!” I yelled, and suddenly a police officer stepped next to her door.

“Is there a problem here ma’am?“ he asked, looking back and forth between us.

“No sir, my step son just won’t get in the car,” she said, smiling at him.

“She killed my dad, I don’t know how but I know she did!” I yelled, pointing at Athena.

“Now son, that is a very serious accusation to make, are you sure that you know what you’re talking about?” He asked.

“No he-“ Athena started but was hushed by the officer.

“I’m gonna need to take you both In for questioning.”

“We walked over to the police car and got in, when we got to the station, they put us in two different rooms. A small man walked into the room I was in and started asking me questions. I explained to him how she was making excuses for my dad not coming home at his usual time, and how her last husband had died under very suspicious circumstances, and how my dad was found in a ditch.

“Is there anywhere you can stay tonight? Maybe a friend's house?” He asked.

“My friend Preston might let me stay,” I said

unsure because we just met.

The police officer from the parking lot took me to my house to pack a bag. We drove to Preston's house and I Waited in the car when the officer walked over to the front door. Preston answered and they talked for a minute and then the officer told me to go inside while he talked to Prestons mom.

We talked and played bored games all night and the next day we hung out in town and on Monday we went to the castle to start training, we actually got armor that fit. At the end of the day I finally got to go home. When I got home I got a call from the police telling me that Athena was guilty for both the murder of my dad and the murder of her last husband. After that I decided to go for a walk in the moonlight, and think about my future, as a knight, with my friend by my side.

The end.

Elliot and The Coyotes

By Shaelynn McGuinness

Once upon a time, there was a bobcat named Elliot. He was the village's detective. Elliot had almost befriended everyone in town. He had solved many simple cases in the past, but little did Elliot know that this next case would change his life. One day Elliot was on a stroll, minding his own business, when there was a big bang that sounded like it came from Ms. Hedgehog's Garden.

Elliot ran in a hurry to find out what had happened. On his way there, he heard another big bang and loud screams coming from her neighbors and people passing by, which made Elliot run faster in a panic.

Elliot finally got to Ms. Hedgehog's garden, finding out that everything was destroyed. There were fruits and vegetables scattered all around the area: smashed, squished, and absolutely obliterated.

He worriedly asked every critter around about what had happened. Everyone who had been there before the bang said they didn't know; all they saw was a flash of light, then an explosion. Elliot had a mystery on his paws.

Him and a few others helped Ms. Hedgehog clean up the damage when, all of a sudden, something grabbed his attention. It was a firecracker. It seemed to have not gone off. He grabbed ahold of it, looking and thinking of someone who would have a firecracker this big. He looked at the bottom of the firecracker in search of any clues on who it belonged to, and wouldn't you know, on the bottom of the firecracker it said "Coyote Chaos". Elliot thought of how stupid it was to put their names on the bottom of something they were using to destroy a garden. Elliot knew who was to blame for setting off the fire cracker.

Elliot headed over to the Coyote's house.

He knocked on the door and waited a minute. Elliot was getting impatient and started banging on the door. When no one answered, Elliot got irritated and snuck in through a vent on the side of the house. When he finally got inside, he started searching for the coyotes but found no one.

Elliot found a note from the Coyotes saying, "You were clever; nonetheless, there is a hint that might be found under the chest. -xoxo Coyotes." Elliot rolled his eyes. He was thinking how silly the coyotes were for leaving a riddle. He dashed over to the chest next to the bed and looked under it, only to find nothing. Those sneaky coyotes left nothing. No smart criminal would give away where they are hiding.

Elliot threw his hat on the ground in frustration, knowing this investigation would be much more challenging than he anticipated.Elliot was left with no choice but to call for some help.

Elliot called his friend " Hey, this is Elliot, I need your help on a case..." Elliot went on to tell Oliver the situation.

"Ok, I'll be there as soon as I can," said Oliver.

Moments later, Elliot heard a knock on the door. He quickly walked over and opened it. It was his friend Oliver. The person he called for help. Oliver had finally gotten to the Coyotes' home. "Hey I'm here, where is this so-called hint?"

"Hey Oliver, the Coyotes left me this riddle-like hint and it was supposed to lead me to another hint under this chest, but either they are stupid and forgot to leave a hint or they are just jerks and lead me on for nothing."

"Hmm, okay lemme get a look," said Oliver. Oliver crouched down and looked under the chest finding nothing, but when he was about to get up he saw a little white piece of paper taped to the top of the bottom side of the chest.

He grabbed it in curiosity and opened it up. Elliot was looking around the room for any other hints or clues about where they might be.

"Elliot! Look what I found under the chest." Elliot dashed over to see what Oliver had found.

"Elliot look, the note says: "good job, you found your hint, the next one will be found near the pit!" They stood there confused, not knowing what the coyotes meant by the pit.

" .... OH, COME ON I KNOW WHERE THE PIT MIGHT BE!"said Elliot as he dashed out of the door. Oliver jumped up from the ground and started following Elliot outside.

Later, Elliot had made it to the pit. Also known as "The Dried-Up Pond." Oliver had finally caught up with Elliot. Oliver followed close by. They looked downward at the pit in fright at how deep it was.

"So... should we Rochambeau to see who goes in first?" Elliot looked at Oliver with a stern face.

"Oliver, you are so childish. Fine." They turned to each other placing their hand in a fist and the other hovering right under it.

"Ro...Cham...BEAU!" They both slammed their hands on their hands and revealed what they had chosen

" Yes," said Elliot. Elliot had chosen rock, and Oliver chose scissors. "Okay, you know what time it is Oliver. Get in the pit." Oliver gave Elliot an annoyed look and started going into the pit slowly.

"Elliot, it's too dark to see anything down here." Elliot headed down the hole following close behind Oliver.

" And this is why you come prepared," said Elliot with a smug look. He had a jar and shook it until it started glowing.

"Oh, fireflies," Oliver said in excitement. Elliot lifted the jar and the walls lit up in a yellowish color. Elliot started searching the depths of the pit while Oliver stayed close behind. Elliot walked up to the wall of the pit in desperation to find the clue.

“Hmmm...what is that?" Elliot called Oliver over and set the jar in Oliver's paws and started digging into the wall.

“Hey..I think I found something.”

Elliot dusted off some dirt from the random object he had found in the wall. It was a box! The box looked to be recently put into the wall as the dirt looked as if it had been tampered with. Elliot opened it in curiosity hoping it was the next hint to the mystery...or treasure, but either way, it had to be at least something useful. Elliot opened the box and found a note and a blue button. The note read, “Wow you understood our hint. If you are so clever, go talk to Trevor."

“Who the heck is Trevor?”

“Oh, I know him. He's the blueberry gardener,” said Elliot as he started crawling back up the pit. “It's getting late, we should go to Trevors in the morning."

“I don't think it's a good idea to wait. What if the Coyotes strike again and we have to do more investigating."

“Oliver... you're so annoying," Elliot sighed.” Okay, fine. Let's go find Trevor."

They both finished crawling out of the pit and started heading toward the direction of Trevor's garden. Before they could get to Trevor’s they had to cross a bridge that was hanging over a river.

“Hey Elliot, can we take another way around the river?”.

“What? Why? We are so close to getting over to Trevor's Garden?”.

“...”

“You're joking.. You're scared of bridges aren't you?”.

"They're just scary because of how high they go up. When I was younger I fell off a bridge and broke my leg on a rock," pleaded Oliver.

" Fine, whatever Oliver. Let's just go around somewhere else." Oliver followed Elliot as they walked through a shallow part of the water in the river.

As Oliver and Elliot walked through the water, Elliot heard a beeping sound coming from the bridge. Elliot turned his head toward the bridge and within a second a huge Boom sounded. The bridge exploded right before Elliot's eyes. Elliot grabbed Oliver by the fur and brought him and himself under the water. Elliot rose up from under the water with a big gasp of air. Oliver came up a few seconds after.

"WHAT THE HECK WAS THAT FOR ELLIOT?!" Oliver shouted

"DID YOU NOT JUST SEE WHAT HAPPENED TO THE BRIDGE?! IT EXPLODED!" Oliver stood there in shock

"Well, I guess it's a good thing we took the long way, am I right?" Elliot gave Oliver a blank stare and shook his head in disappointment. They finally started walking across the river.

They had finally made it across the river, even though it took them a half an hour. They started making their way over to Trevor's garden.

"Hey, is that it up there?" asked Oliver. Elliot and Oliver started walking toward an abandoned building covered in weeds and brush.

"Uhm, are you sure this is Trevor's garden? It looks like an abandoned graveyard or something." Elliot nodded with a nervous expression and started looking around to see if anyone was in the building

"Yep, this is Trevor's place, but Trevor is nowhere to be seen."

Elliot sat on a log, stumped on where Trevor is. "Oliver, I don't know what we are gonna do. Trevor is nowhere to be seen and the bridge over the river is in pieces and the water is rising as we speak and we will be stuck over here." Oliver sat down next to Elliot.

"Elliot we can't just sit around feeling sorry for ourselves because we can't find Trevor. We need to get up and not give up." Elliot let out a sigh and stood up

"Okay, yes, we can't give up. I know, but still we have no idea where to find him. For all we know he's probably dead."

"Oh my god, I know where to go." Oliver said. Elliot started to follow Oliver down a little path in a part of the forest. Oliver had led Elliot and himself to a graveyard. It seemed this graveyard hadn't been visited in years.

"Did you really just bring us to a graveyard?" Oliver whispered in a worried tone.

"Duh, I mean why else would Trevor's garden be in shambles and the building decaying? If Trevor really loved his garden, he wouldn't let it get that bad. Which hints, he's most likely dead."

Oliver just looked at Elliot with a distraught face and started walking around looking for Trevor's possible grave. Oliver started searching as well. They searched for hours. Elliot started losing hope and looked at one more grave. It was covered in moss and weeds. Elliot wiped some of the dirt off with his paw to see the name. It was Trevor's grave!

"Oliver, I found it!"

Oliver dashed over to the tomb. They stood there not knowing what to do now.

"So..where do we look for the hint?" asked Oliver. Elliot started looking around the grave seeing if there was maybe a box or a note that would lead them to their next hint.

"Hmm, I'm not seeing anything around the grave." Elliot and Oliver stood before his grave and slowly looked down at the ground.

"They wouldn't put it..in his grave..right?"inquired Oliver with a nervous laugh. Elliot went and grabbed a shovel he had found on the ground.

"There's only one way to find out. Oliver, you keep a lookout to see if anyone's coming."

Oliver gave Elliot a disgusted face and started looking away. Elliot started to dig. He had dug for a good 5 minutes and had finally hit something. Elliot cleared off the rest of the dirt and it appeared to be a box. Elliot took off the lid of the box. There was no body, but there was a note.

The note said," Wow, you took deep precautions to find us, even digging up a grave. If you are so bright you will stop here and behave, but if you are so eager you'll find us near the eagle. P.S. We know most of this doesn't rhyme."

"Okay now, this one I can tell is gonna be hard. Where the heck are we gonna find an eagle? There are no eagles in this part of the forest." Oliver came back to see what Elliot found.

"Elliot what does the note say?". Elliot passed over the paper to Oliver so he could read it.

"What? What do they mean eagle? There are no eagles here?" said Oliver with a confused face.

"That's what I said!". Elliot stood there thinking.

"I know earlier you insisted on staying longer

Oliver but, I think we should go home, get some rest, and meet back over here tomorrow."

Oliver let out a sigh.

"Ok, I'll meet you here at sunrise?".

"Sounds good, thanks Oliver." Elliot started walking away when he heard that beeping sound he had heard when the bridge exploded.HE felt the ground began to vibrate . It felt as if the ground had a heart beat. He turned around and saw a trail of explosions coming toward him.

Oliver was standing right in the path of the explosions.

"OLIVER WATCH OUT!" Cried Elliot. Oliver turned around and within a second a bomb exploded right next to him. Oliver screamed and was launched across the graveyard and slammed into a grave. The whole moment felt like it was in slow motion, it felt like the world was just spinning uncontrollably.

"OLIVER!" Elliot shouted in a panic.

Elliot ran over to Oliver's body lying next to the grave.

"Oliver! Come on, wake up!". Elliot started shaking him and started to look for his heartbeat. Elliot's eyes started to water in panic. Elliot kept shaking Oliver, trying to wake him up. Elliots heart was racing. It felt like Elliot was stabbed.This pain was something Elliot had experienced before. Which he was not prepared for. Definitely not this time.

Oliver slowly fluttered open his eyes and let out a cough. Elliot let out a sigh of relief and wiped his eyes . Elliot quickly swooped down and gave Oliver a tight hug."I thought I lost you there."Said Elliot, tears still falling from his eyes. Oliver let out a snicker

"You can't get rid of me.. But you can get me to a hospital." Said Oliver with a faint giggle.

Elliot picked up Oliver and hurriedly headed back to town. The next day Elliot visits Oliver in the Hospital.

"Hey! How are you doing? Does it hurt as much as it did yesterday?".

"It definitely doesn't hurt as much, I'm just a little sore. The doctor said I broke some ribs, a leg, and fractured my paw."

Elliot frowned.

"I'm so sorry Oliver, I should've never brought you with me, I'm the reason you're hurt."

"Elliot, no one would have known I was gonna get hurt, you shouldn't blame yourself for something uncontrollable."

"...So what do we do now? The Coyotes are still out there and now that you can't be there anymore it's gonna be a lot more challenging."

"Elliot, I know you, you can do this. It is up to you to keep everyone safe."

"Thanks, Oliver, maybe something will come up and will lead to them. I have to go and do some research, I'll visit you tomorrow, Ok?"

"Okay, but, before you leave, I might know where they are."

Oliver's words grabbed Elliot's attention

"you know where they might be?".

Oliver sat up in his bed.

"Yes, you know how in the hint they said we will find them near an eagle, well what if they mean Eagle point?". Elliot stood there in awe.

"Oh my god, why didn't I think of that. It's so obvious."

“Thank you, Oliver, I have to go get prepared”. Said Elliot as he started speed walking out of the room.

“Wait, Elliot!”. Elliot stopped right in front of the door.

“You need to be careful. You know they are willing to hurt you. You know what happened to me, They tried blowing us up!”.

Elliot turned around and said,

“I promise I'll be careful." And walked out of the room. The next day Elliot started packing for his adventure.

“Ok, I have the food, water, map, med kit, weapons… Ok, I think I've got everything!”. Elliot had now started his journey up to the top of The Eagle point. After hours He had climbed far and wide,Through bush spikes, high cliffs, animal caves, and more. Until he eventually made it close to the top of the mountain. Elliot was climbing on some branches when all of a sudden he heard a beeping sound. Elliot's Eyes grew bigger . “Aw crap."

The next second there was a boom right above Elliot, and rocks started tumbling down at an alarming speed. Elliot started to panic and ha accidentally let go of the branch and tumbled down a small way and finally reached out and grabbed a branch. Elliot waited a moment and started climbing back up again. Another explosion went by right above Elliot again. The second explosion had caused a landslide and rocks came plummeting down the cliff.

“Give me a break!” Elliot yelled He quickly climbed to a little bat cave and waited for the rocks to stop falling. An hour passed and Elliot finally poked his head out to make sure the coast was clear. When he saw no more rocks falling he climbed out of the cave and continued his journey up the mountain. Elliot had finally reached the top of the mountain 'AKA' the Eagle Point.

Elliot picked himself up and looked around. "Where are they? I know I'm on the right mountain, they wouldn't just have bombs here for fun... or would they?". Elliot started looking around when he saw something in the corner of his eye. It was a note, it said:

"Out for lunch." Elliot stared at the paper

"I swear to god, I did not just climb up a huge mountain, almost explode and die just for them to be out for lunch."

As Elliot was crumpling up the note he heard some footsteps behind him.

"Oh, you didn't waste your time for nothing.." Said the mysterious person behind Elliot. Elliot quickly turned around and saw the person who he heard speak was no other than... TREVOR.

Elliot let out a gasp. The three Coyotes walked out from behind Trevor and stood behind him.

"We meet again, Elliot."

"Why are you doing this? What about your garden, why did you leave it, why did you blow up Ms.Hedgehogs garden?". Said Elliot with a shaky voice.

"I BLEW UP HER GARDEN BECAUSE SHE DESERVED IT!... A long time ago me and Ms. Hedgehog were dating, we had been dating for over three years. She wanted to have a garden and grow blueberries and name it after me. We grew closer and I finally proposed to her and all went well and we had our wedding planned all out. Sadly two weeks before our wedding I finally came home from work to find her in bed with someone else. I stood there in shock when something just snapped, I grabbed my pocket knife and flung him out of the bed. I pinned him to the ground and continuously stabbed him."

Elliots jaw dropped. "When I turned to look at Mrs.Hedgehog, I saw her face that was full of fear. I just turned around and walked out. I went into hiding after that, planning on what to do to get revenge." Said Trevor. Elliot looked at Trevor with a disgusted face. "I have gotten revenge on everyone who has ever wronged me in any way." "Elliot looked down to the ground.

"That is no reason to hurt people or destroy their things! Tell me why you thought doing any of this was a good idea, or a way to cope with your trauma?".

"Because I said it was." Said Trevor giving Elliot a stern look.

"Okay, then answer the rest of the questions I asked."

"You really wanna know why I left that stupid garden? I left it because I was bankrupt, and you and your stupid mom were the only people who had still bought berries from me. But when your mom passed away I made no sales. So when I heard the Coyotes' were hiring a new boss I hopped onto the deal. Now after I joined them I'm making 100x more than I ever did at that stupid blueberry farm. ". Elliot stood there in shock.

"So you're saying instead of promoting your business and finding ways to make it more popular you thought becoming a criminal was the only answer?". Said Elliot.

“Hmm...Hmmm.. let me think... OF COURSE DUH!

I have robbed almost everyone in this little town and you and your little friend are the only people left, and I know you're not broke, like come on you're the town's detective.``. Elliot took a step back.

“You're not getting anything from me, the only thing you're getting is a trip behind bars." Said Elliot in an aggravated voice. Trevor laughed.

“You think you can take me down, I'd like to see you try." Trevor looked over his shoulder “take care of him, boys." Trevor backed up and the three coyotes walked forward

“This is gonna be a piece of cake."

Said one of the coyotes as he grabbed a remote from one of the other coyotes' hands.

Elliot kneeled and grabbed something out of his bag.

“Let's just get this over with Elliot!”. Said one of the coyotes’.

Right after he said that bombs started going off around Elliot. Elliot started to dodge them and once he escaped he looked at one of the coyote's hands and realized he was controlling the bombs with a little remote.

“I have to get rid of that remote to stop them!”.

The coyotes set off another round of bombs and Elliot started running around. After the round of explosions stopped Elliot grabbed a circular ball out of his bag and threw it right in front of the coyotes. It made a tiny explosion and let out loads of smoke. Elliot ran over to the coyote and tried grabbing the remote from the coyote's hand.

The coyote started fighting back. The other two

coyotes started fighting as well by pulling Elliot's fur, pushing, punching, and even biting. Elliot shoved his way through both of the coyotes and reached out to grab the remote. Trevor came in and slammed Elliot to the ground. Trevor then grabbed Elliot by his neck tuff and walked over to the edge of the cliff. Elliot started shaking in fear and tried to get loose from Trevors grip.

"Oh Elliot.. we could have been friends, we wouldn't have to be going through this right now if you would have just left me alone, and minded your own business instead of snooping in places where you shouldn't have been. Look what you're making me do because of your actions." Said Trevor as he stretched his hand out farther off of the cliff.

Elliot started to panic

"WAIT TREVOR, PLEASE DON'T DO THIS. I'M BEGGING YOU." Shouted Elliot.Trevor looked Elliot straight in the eyes.

"It was nice knowing you Elliot." Said Trevor as he tossed Elliot off of the ledge. Elliot let a blood-curdling scream while falling to his doom. After Trevor had let go of Elliot he turned around and walked toward the Coyotes. "Search his belongings, he must have something good in that bag of his."

"Yes Boss." Said the coyotes.

As Elliot was falling he saw a bush of vines and started pushing himself toward them. He grabbed the vines and held on for dear life. He hung there astonished and saw the vines slowly snap in half. He scrambled up and sat on a ledge still in shock from what happened. He looked up to see how far he fell. It was only about 30 feet, so Elliot hurried and started heading back up the mountain. Elliot hid behind a bush once he finally made it to the top.

"Alrighty, boys, here's your cut for this job." Trever handed the Coyotes a sum of cash and goods.

"What the heck is this? You promised us almost triple what we made last time!". Trevor glared at them.

"Well that's too bad buddy, life is unfair. Plus I said maybe triple it was never guaranteed." Said Trevor as he started counting his cash. The coyotes started growling at Trevor.

"Oh give me a break, this job is hard enough on me and here you guys are being ungrateful for what I'm giving you ." Elliot started slowly sneaking up behind the one coyote that still had the remote in his hand.

Elliot reached his paw out and his fingers were an inch away from the remote when tripped on a rock and made him lose his balance. Before he could fall he caught himself, but it was too late. When Elliot was wobbling he accidentally touched one of the coyotes' paws. The coyote turned around and yelled, "Hey! What do you think you're doing?! You're supposed to be dead!". Said Trevor

Elliot stood there for a second and darted forward and punched the coyote talking to Trevor.. The coyote collapsed and his brothers turned to look at Elliot. They turned around and darted toward Elliot. Elliot had grabbed something out of his pocket, it was another circular firecracker.

Elliot slammed it on the ground and darted toward the coyotes as they stood there coughing and waving the smoke away. Elliot tackled the coyotes and wrestled on the ground fighting for the remote.

They tossed and turned until Elliot finally got the remote in his grasp. He stood up and snapped the remote in half.

Trevor gave Elliot an aggravated look. “You think snapping a remote is gonna stop us? You're funny." Trevor started walking toward Elliot. Elliot took a step back.

“No, maybe that won't stop you, but they will." Said Elliot as he pointed upward. Trevor and the coyotes looked up to see nothing. Trevor was about to put his head back down when all of a sudden someone pounced on him. It was a police officer. Trevor was pinned to the ground.

“WHAT THE HELL IS GOING ON, LET ME GO!”.

Said Trevor while he was wiggling trying to escape. “ You have the right to stay silent until proven guilty in a court of law." Said one of the officers as they lifted Trevor up and put him in handcuffs.

More policemen arose from the bushes and obtained the coyotes. Elliot grinned as he watched them being put in handcuffs knowing that he won.

Elliot turned around to see Oliver standing there with a cane staring at Elliot. Oliver smiled and waved, Elliot walked over

“What the heck are you doing here?”.said Elliot as his smile grew bigger

“Why do you think there are police here?”. Said Oliver with a smug look.

“I don't know, I thought they kinda just followed me here”. Said Elliot .

Oliver's jaw dropped. “I'm just kidding dude!”. Elliot started looking Oliver up and down.

“How the heck did you get up here in crutches?”. Oliver gave Elliot another disappointed look.

“Don't you see the helicopter right there?”. Elliot looked over at the helicopter.

“Oh."

“Now come on, let's get you to a clinic, looks like they knocked you up pretty good." Said Oliver as he started walking to the chopper

Elliot stopped in his tracks and looked up.The moon had finally risen and the moonlight was shining upon him. He took a deep breath and got into the Helicopter knowing he had finally brought peace to his village. Elliot helped Oliver get in, and they set off back to town.

Over the next several months Elliot and many others helped rebuild Ms. Hedgehogs' garden and everything else the coyotes destroyed. Oliver's wounds healed and he went on to restore Trevor's old garden and plant all sorts of fruits and vegetables. Trevor and the coyotes went on to go to jail and they got a sentence of 30 years of prison for second degree murder, an attempted murder, vandalism of others property and theft, Criminal possession of a weapon, and way more but i am too lazy to name the rest.

Elliot planned on moving to a bigger city to become a full-time detective and take on bigger cases. Although Elliot would miss Oliver and all of his friends he knew he needed to move on to become more independent and strong.

Elliot had packed all of his bags and was about to get on the train to leave when he heard a voice yell Elliot's name. Elliot turned around and Oliver came up and hugged Elliot tight. They both shared a long and very awkward hug.

Oliver let go of Elliot

"Do you really have to go, you could just stay here with us!". Elliot grinned and nodded his head

" yes I need to go, there are people out there who need me."

"But I need you! You're my best friend, What am I gonna do without you?". Said Oliver

"You are gonna make new friends and your business is gonna do amazing. The best part is, you're not gonna need me because you're capable of doing anything". Said Elliot as he slowly started getting on the train.

Oliver waved as Elliot got on the train and the doors closed. Elliot put his paw on the window and watched Oliver as he slowly started to disappear out of sight as the train started moving. Elliot sat down. He sat on the bus for hours thinking about all the memories he had made and all of the friends he had with him by his side and just everything that had happened. Elliot had drifted off into a slumber when he had finally woke up. He had arrived in his new town. Elliot got off and made his way to the police station. He walked through the doors and went up to the front desk. "Hello ma'am, My name is Elliot woods, I am a detective for woods burrow county. I would like to sign up for training to become the chief of detectives."

The woman behind the desk sighed.

" And what do you think makes you qualified to be put up in such a high rank?". Said the woman crossing her arms.

"Oh If you do not believe me deserving of such a high rank, let me tell you a little story called... "Elliot And The Coyotes."

The End.

Porcelain

By Kaitlyn Ferguson

Set in the 1910s a woman named Catherine takes her friends and her maid on a cruise. Then something very unexpected happens. Murders begin happening. As her friends start mysteriously ending up dead, the remaining friends begin trying to figure out who is behind the murders.

Catherine was frantically looking through her suitcase. She was looking for her veil.

"Mary, have you seen my veil? I could have sworn I had packed it." Marie came into the bedroom.

"No, I have not. Have you lost it?"

"It appears so." Catherine replied. Suddenly there was a knock at the door. Marie quickly went to open it. One of the friends Catherine was going on the cruise with, Asbel was there.

"Are you ready yet? The tea party is about to begin." Catherine turned to look at her.

"No, it seems I have misplaced my veil."

"Are you serious Catherine?" Asbel said. "How could you misplace something like that?"

Catherine had a worried look on her face. "I really don't know."

"Well whatever." Asbel said."Just come to the tea party." Catherine stood up.

"Well fine. I suppose it's not that big of a deal." Catherine touched up her makeup and went to the tea party.

Catherine showed up at the party a bit early, So did her friend Rose. Rose was leaning on the balcony looking out on the water. Catherine joined her. "I'm glad you went with us on this cruise Catherine." Rose said. "I know it's a bit sudden since your husband recently passed. Nonetheless I hope you still have fun."

Catherine looked at Rose. "Thank you." Clover walked up to the table and set some pastries and tea down. "This looks great," said Rose as she admired the desserts that were on the table.

"Thank you, I hope you enjoy your party." Clover replied. "Let me know if you need anything." She walked off. Asbel, Alex, and Elliot walked up to the table.

"Well you two are quite early." Elliot said.

Everyone sat down at the fancy cruise ship tables. Catherine poured everyone their tea. Rose sat next to Catherine.

Asbel picked up a pastry and began to eat it. "This is really good," she said. Rose nodded her head in agreement.

"Did you hear?" Asbel said.

"About what." Rose said as she set down her tea cup.

"About Diana and her husband." Asbel replied. "They seem to be going through something." Asbel took a quick sip of her tea.

"I saw Diana and her husband arguing in the middle of a restaurant! It seems that Diane has been disloyal to him." Rose had a bit of a shocked look on her face. "They always seemed like such a happy couple though."

"I don't know," Catherine piped in. "Diana was always complaining about her husband."

"Well isn't that normal?" Asbel said. "You ALWAYS complained about your husband Catherine."

"You shouldn't talk about Catherine's relationship with her husband while she's grieving Asbel." Rose said.

"Well I was simply stating a fact." Asbel replied. Everyone sat in silence.

Suddenly a horrific scream was heard coming from the kitchen. Everyone stood up and made their way to where the scream was heard. Clover was standing in front of the freezer seemingly paralyzed.

"What happened!?" Rose exclaimed. Rose's gaze suddenly shifted to the floor. Everyone else caught up to her.

"What's wrong!?" said Catherine. Catherine quickly looked down to see one of the cooks dead on the floor. Her body was almost completely frozen. Everyone stood in absolute shock. The other chef was standing next to Clover in shock. One of the security guards came to see what was happening. "

Everyone step back." The guard said. More security guards showed up and escorted everyone out of the kitchen. The guards made Clover stay behind to question her. Catherine began walking Rose to her room.

"Are you going to be okay sleeping alone tonight?" Catherine asked.

"Yes, I should be fine." Rose replied.

"Well alright, I'm going to go back to my room now then." Catherine said.

'I'll see you in the morning." Catherine walked back to her room. When she walked in Marie was sitting on her bed looking down at her feet and twiddling her thumbs. "You always find a way to cause problems for me." Catherine muttered. "I really can't have a nice vacation without you losing your self control." Marie didn't say anything and continued to look down at her feet. "Why would you do this after I brought you here?" Catherine continued.

"I'm sorry." Marie muttered.

Catherine sighed. "You know I do care about you." It's just sometimes..." Catherine didn't finish her sentence. "Whatever it's fine, let's just go to bed and deal with it in the morning.

The next morning Catherine was walking along the side of the boat and encountered Rose. "I'm just so confused," she said, "Why would someone kill some random chef?"

"I'm not sure." Catherine replied. "It was

probably one of the staff members."

"Maybe." Rose replied.. "I bet you it was the chef that served our tea."

"Well I doubt that." Asbel said from behind them. Rose and Catherine turned to look at her. "The other chef had been with her all night and was there when the body was found."

Asbel leaned on the railing. "It was probably a crew member she had some history with. There are very few people other than crew members on this boat. I doubt some random person just decided to kill a chef."

"I'll be right back." Catherine said. "I need to freshen up." She walked off.

As she was walking to her room she went to the lobby to see if Marie was there. When she opened the door there she was laying on one of the couches. She sat up as soon as she saw Catherine. "Why not go check out the rest of the ship?" Catherine asked. "It's better than moping around all day." Catherine sat next to her. After a moment of silence Catherine asked "What were you doing wandering around in the kitchen anyways."

"I was checking out the dining room and somehow found my way into the kitchen. I was just kind of wandering. I'm not sure what I was even thinking." Marie looked down at her feet. "I just saw her there and I don't know why I just shoved her in the freezer, I felt like I needed to. She seemed oddly familiar, something about her just.. I don't know"

"Well just try not to worry about it." Catherine said. "We're almost to land once we get there it'll all be over."

Rose and Elliot opened the door. "Me and Elliot are going to check out the crime scene, you should come with us." Marie turned to look at Catherine.

"Why not." Catherine replied as she sat up and walked over to them.

Catherine, Rose and Elliot soon showed up to the scene. The body had been taken away by the guards. There was a chalk outline where the body had been.

"Elliot look!" said Rose.

Elliot turned to look in the direction she was pointing. There was a piece of cloth under the door to the freezer. Elliot crouched down to pick it up. It was a black cotton fabric that was clearly torn off. "Was the chef wearing a black dress?" Elliot asked.

"No she wasn't." Rose replied.

"It must be the killers then." Elliot said. He put the piece of cloth into his pocket.

"What are you guys doing?" Asbel exclaimed as she walked into the kitchen.

"I saw you guys in the window."

"We were just taking a look at the crime scene." Rose said.

"We found this." Elliot said as he showed her the piece of cloth.

"Where'd you find this?" Asbel asked.

"It was under the door to the freezer." Elliot replied.

"The killer must have gotten their dress stuck under the door when they were closing it." Rose said. "What do you think Catherine?"

Catherine turned to look at Rose. "Perhaps."

"Hold onto that piece of cloth Elliot." Asbel said. "We just need to find whose dress that came from."

"I'm going to get ready for dinner." Catherine

announced. “I'm assuming you guys are going, correct?”

“I'll be there!” Rose said.

“Me and Alex are coming.” Elliot said. “I'll be there as well.” Asbel piped in.

“Well, I'll see you guys there.” Catherine said As she started making her way to her room.

Catherine was about to turn the corner and head to her room when she overheard Elliot talking to Marie.

“I couldn't help but notice you seemed to have torn your dress,” Elliot said.

“Oh yeah… I ripped it while I was walking on the deck of the ship.” Marie replied.

Catherine turned the corner. “Hello Elliot,” she said.

“Oh hello Catherine.”

“Is Alex going to be at the dinner?” Catherine asked,

“Yes he will be there.” Elliot replied.

“Oh yeah! I lost my wedding ring near the deck and I need help finding it.” Catherine said.

“Oh, alright.” Elliot replied.

Catherine and Elliot began walking to the deck. Catherine and Elliot walked to the deck and started looking for Catherine’s ring.

“I doubt we'll be able to find it.” Elliot said. “I probably fell through the cracks.”

Catherine stared down at her feet. “I suppose you're right… but it doesn't hurt to look. I probably won't find it, but I still feel the need to try.”

After a few minutes of searching Catherine leaned on the rail and looked at the ocean. Elliot stood next to her. “I know that ring meant a lot to you.” Elliot said. Catherine turned away. “But, don’t be too upset about it." Elliot continued. "We're going to have a lot of fun on this cruise I'm sure." Catherine seemed upset. "We took this vacation to celebrate our friendship. We sure wouldn't want you to be sad the entire trip." Elliot said as he leaned onto the railing. Catherine seemed to have a sad yet angry look on her face.

"It's fine. I'm sure I'll manage."

Elliot turned to look at her. "Catherine, how long have you had that maid?"

Catherine quickly turned her head to face Elliot. "About five years… why?"

"Well I don't know she's been acting strange ever since we got here. I mean It's strange you even brought her in the first place." Elliot said.

"Well I didn't want her roaming around the house." Catherine replied.

"Well I suppose that makes sense." Elliot said.

Catherine took her arms off the railing. "Well I'm going back to my room to get ready for dinner."

"Alright." Elliot said. "I'll see you then."

Catherine began walking off when she suddenly stopped. Elliot's back was this facing her he was still looking at the ocean. She quietly turned to him. She was standing right behind him. Catherine retracted her arms and pushed Elliot's back as hard as she could. Elliot nearly fell off as his torso was pressed against the top of the rail and his feet were in the air. He began to try to regain his balance and bring himself back onto the deck when Catherine pushed his feet and he screamed as he fell into the water. There was a big splash.

After a few seconds she saw blood begin to form from under the boat. Elliot had gotten stuck under the boat's propellers. Catherine stood there for a second and watched the blood take up a small portion of the water. Strands of her hair were blowing in the wind. Suddenly she reached into the pocket of her dress and pulled out her wedding ring. She looked at it for a moment before looking back at the ocean. She raised the hand she was holding her ring in and threw it as far as she could into the ocean.

Catherine walked into the door to her room. "Did something happen? I heard screaming coming from the deck." Marie said.

Catherine looked at her. "Elliot is dead." She said with blank expressions.

"What?" Marie said, a bit frightened.

"He knew that you killed that stupid chef. No need to thank me." Catherine said as she looked in the mirror. She began touching up her makeup. Marie was staring at her. "What time is it?" Catherine asked.

Marie turned to look at the clock. "It's 4:50," She replied. "I should get going soon then."

Asbel, Alex and Rose were sitting at the table. "Catherine and Elliot seem to be running quite late," said Alex.

"Yeah they said they would be here," Asbel replied.

Clover soon came over to take their order. "What would you like to eat tonight?" she said as she whipped out a clipboard.

"We need just a few more minutes, we're still waiting for two more people," Rose said.

"I wonder where they could be.." Alex said.

"Clover, could you look for Catherine and Elliot?" Asbel asked.

"Why of course. I'll be right back." Clover replied

as she walked away.

"I wonder what's keeping them," Rose said.

Suddenly Catherine walked over to their table. "Sorry I was a bit late. I was touching up my makeup."

"Well Clover just went to look for you and Elliot, have you seen him?" Rose said.

"No, I haven't seen him since the tea party." Catherine replied.

"That's odd," Asbel said. Suddenly a waitress began to walk to their table.

"Have you all decided what you would like as an appetizer?" she asked.

"Yes, we would like the caviar." Rose replied. Suddenly a group of people near the front of the restaurant huddled near the door. Soon more and more people were joining the group.

"What's going on?" Catherine asked.

"I'm not sure," Rose replied. Rose got up to see what was happening and the others followed. "What's happening?" Rose asked a person who was standing near the door.

"The security guards are talking about how someone fell overboard," the woman replied.

Asbel, Alex, Rose and Catherine went outside to see what happened. There were security guards looking around this certain area near the edge of the boat. They walked over to the railing and saw a leg on top of the water. There were drops of blood and fabric along the side of the ship.

"Look!" Alex exclaimed as he pointed to a pair of cufflinks that were snagged on a piece of metal along the side of the ship.

"Those are Elliots aren't they?" Rose said.

"Yeah," Alex replied.

Everyone went back to their respective rooms. As Catherine was walking to her room Alex began to walk next to her.

"Oh, hello Alex," Catherine said.

"Hi," Alex replied.

"How are you? Are you going to be okay?" Catherine asked.

"I guess. I'm still trying to process everything." Alex replied. Catherine and Alex walked in silence for a moment. When Catherine was about to enter her room Alex interrupted her, "Hey.... weren't you the last one to talk to Elliot? I saw you walking with him about an hour before we had dinner."

Catherine sat in silence for a second not knowing what to say. "Well yes. Why?"

"No reason," Alex said.

"Do you think I killed Elliot?" Catherine said with a sad tone.

"Well, nO. I was just wondering," Alex said.

Catherine looked at him for a moment before shutting her door. Marie was sleeping on her bed. Catherine walked over to the mirror and began to remove her makeup and accessories. She took her long hair out of the bun she had put it in. It fell down to the middle of her back. She went to the bathroom to take a bath and change into her nightgown.

Catherine woke up in the middle of the night. Marie was still asleep in the bed next to her. Catherine sat up and got out of her bed. She put on her slippers and walked out of her room shutting the door behind her quietly. She walked along the halls of the ship and out to the balcony. She put her hand on the white railing.

Suddenly Alex stood next to her.

"Alex! What are you doing up this late?" Catherine asked.

"Couldn't sleep," Alex replied while looking down at the floor below them.

"Yeah me neither," Catherine said in a soft voice. "Do you really think I killed Elliot?"

"Will you please let go of that?" Alex said. "I didn't mean what I said." Catherine didn't say anything. "You know Elliot and I were close. It's just hard to fathom what happened to him," Alex said. "I mean I know you didn't know him that well."

"I knew Elliot!" Catherine snapped back. "This affects me too, you know. Rose and Asbel are also devastated." There was a cold silence in the air. "It's freezing out here.." Catherine said.

"Go back to bed then." Alex replied. Catherine took her hands off the railing. "Fine, maybe I will."

Catherine began walking away. She stopped for a second before turning around. Alex's back was facing her. She stood there for a second. Alex had thought she had left. She looks to her right to see a conveniently placed plank of wood. She picked it up as silently as possible. She walked closer to Alex, lifted the plank over her shoulder and hit his head with it.

Alex was knocked unconscious. His body launched halfway onto the rail, his torso was pressing against it. Catherine took his legs and pushed him off the edge. His body fell and crashed onto one of the tables on the deck below them.

The next day, people were talking about what happened in the halls which woke up Catherine. "Of course these people are gossiping right outside my door."

"They're talking about what happened to Alex

miss," Marie said.

"Well whatever they're being awfully loud," Catherine said as she rolled out of bed.

"Are there any plans for today miss?" Marie asked.

"We are supposed to have dinner tonight," Catherine replied. "I'm going to take a bath. Can you prepare my clothes for me?"

"Yes miss." Marie replied. While Catherine was taking her bath Marie heard a knock at the door. She opened it to see Rose.

"Hello Marie. Is Catherine there?" Rose asked with a worried voice.

"She's currently taking a bath." Marie replied.

"I'll wait here for her then," said as she walked in and took a seat on Catherine's bed.

"Marie!" Catherine yelled from the bathroom. "Hand me my clothes please!"

"Okay." Marie said as she grabbed her dress and handed it to Catherine who was sticking her hand out the door. After a few minutes Catherine came out of the bathroom.

"Catherine!" Rose said as she stood up.

"Oh hello Rose, is something the matter?"

"Alex he....They found him on the deck last night. He seemed to have fallen from the balcony," Rose said.

"Oh dear, is he alright?" Catherine said worryingly.

"I'm afraid not... Alex is dead."

Catherine's eyes widened. "Oh god."

"Why does this keep happening?" Rose said. "First Elliot and now Alex. Why would someone do this?" Rose looked up at Catherine. "I just want to go home," Rose said as she hugged Catherine.

"Hey I'm sure we'll be fine.."

"One of us is probably next," Rose said.

"Oh don't say that.," Catherine said. "It's going to be alright, we'll find out who's behind this."

Rose pulled herself away from Catherine. "I don't want anything bad to happen to you, or Asbel."

Catherine sighed, "Are you coming to the diner tonight?"

"Yes," Rose replied.

Catherine, Rose and Asbel stayed in their respective rooms until it was about time for dinner.

Catherine was ready so she decided to take a walk along the deck. The moon was already out. While she was taking her walk she came across Rose. "Oh hello," Catherine said.

"Hi." Rose replied.

"How are you doing?" Catherine asked.

"I'm okay, I suppose," Rose replied.

"You seem upset," Catherine said.

"I just feel lost about Alex and Elliot." Rose said as she turned around, leaned on the railing and looked up at the moon.

Catherine was behind Rose. She reached into her pocket. She waited a second before slowly taking a dagger out of her dress pocket. She waited a second to make sure Rose didn't turn around. She held the dagger near the back of Rose's stomach and stabbed her. Rose started to hold her stomach before falling backwards onto Catherine. Catherine held her in her arms and quickly dragged her to her room. She opened the door and threw her onto the bed.

"Oh my god!" Marie yelled. "What the hell!"

"Calm down." Catherine said.

"Why'd you bring that in here!?" Marie exclaimed.

"Because I have plans for it." Catherine replied.

"What.." Marie said.

Catherine picked Rose up and took her to the bathroom. She laid her in the tub. Marie followed her to the bathroom. Catherine took the dagger out of her pocket again. She undressed Rose and started cutting her body into pieces.

Marie stood there and watched. She separated the ribs from the rest of the body. She started preparing the ribs as if they were intended to be eaten. She separated them from the rest of the body and laid them down on a towel. She wrapped the ribs up in the towel and walked out of the bathroom. Marie followed her.

"Put these in the freezer." Catherine said.

"What," Marie replied. "Why?"

"Just do it and don't get caught," Catherine said as she handed Marie the towel.

"Alright," Marie said. She walked out the door.

Marie quickly walked down the halls trying her best not to reveal what was inside the towel. She quickly made her way to the restaurant. "Why would she make me do this.. I'm not good at sneaking around," Marie whispered to herself. She made her way to the door to the kitchen that was next to the bathrooms.

Clover and the other chef were both busy with something that was in the oven. Marie quickly made a run for the freezer. She quietly opened and closed the door. She spotted a shelf that she could place the ribs on. She unwrapped them. They were still very bloody. She tried her best not to get it on her hands. She placed the ribs on the shelf.

Suddenly the door started to open. Marie looked around for a place to hide. She decided to tuck herself in a shelf behind various dead animals that were hanging from the wall. Clover walked in the door. Marie's hands clenched the towel.

"I can't believe this," Clover said. She seemed to be looking for something. Marie watched as she walked past her. She clenched the towel even more, squeezing the blood out of it. Clover reached her hand for the body that was hiding Marie.

"What did they order again?" Clover yelled.

"The beef tenderloin!" The other chef yelled back. Clover took her hand away from the hook and grabbed some meat on a shelf on the other side of the room. Clover walked out and closed the door.

Marie sighed in relief. She got up and peeked out the door to see where they were. Clover was busy cutting the beef with the other chef. Marie made a run for it. Her hands were bloody from squeezing the towel. She dashed out the door and out of the kitchen. She leaned her body against the wall beside the door to the kitchen. Then she ran again. She covered her bloody hands with the towel. She ran across the halls and made it back to her room. She quickly went in to shut the door behind her.

"Back already?" Catherine said. She was reading a magazine while sitting on the chair next to the window. Marie sighed and went to the bathroom to wash her hands.

"Marie, why don't you join me and Asbel for dinner tonight?" Catherine said without looking up from her magazine.

"Me? Oh. I couldn't. I don't even have a dress to wear," Marie replied.

“Oh nonsense. You can borrow one of mine,” Catherine said.

“Really?” said Marie.

“Why of course.” Catherine said as she reached into her bag and pulled out one of her dresses. It was a purple and black dress.

“Thank you.” Marie said as she went to change. Catherine went back to her magazine. A few minutes later Marie came out of the bathroom in the dress.

“Your hair is still a mess,” Catherine said. “Come on.” Catherine grabbed Marie’s arm and dragged her into the bathroom again. She picked up her brush off the counter. She stood Marie in front of the mirror and started doing her hair.

After brushing it out she put it in a braid. She pulled two strands of hair out of the braid and in front of her face. “Alright I suppose we're ready to go then,” Catherine said. Marie nodded. Catherine grabbed her purse and left the room with Marie.

Catherine and Marie met Asbel at their table.

“Have you seen Rose?” Asbel asked as they sat down.

“She said she wasn't feeling well,” Catherine said. A waitress walked up to them.

“Are you three ready to order?” “

Have you chosen yet?” Catherine asked Asbel.

“Not yet.”

The waitress put her pen back in her pocket,“I’ll come back in a bit then!” She walked away.

Asbel was looking at the menu. “Have you two decided what you want?” Asbel asked.

“Yes we have,” Catherine replied. “We were thinking of getting the ribs.”

“Ribs? Those are quite messy though. It would

be embarrassing," Asbel said.

"They are 'fall off the bone ribs' We can eat them with a fork." Catherine said.

Asbel put her menu down, "Ribs do sound pretty good. But, I was thinking of getting the steak."

"You always have steak Asbel you should switch it up a bit!" Catherine said.

"All right.." Asbel said as she put her menu at the end of the table.

The waitress came back around again. "Are you guys ready to order?"

"Yes, we are." Catherine said. "We are all going to have ribs.. And how about the caviar as an appetizer!"

Marie scrunched her face up in disgust.

"Alright," the waitress said, "that will be ready in just a moment!" She walked away.

"So Rose isn't feeling well?" Asbel asked.

"Yes she came to my room saying she was sick. I don't blame her.. With everything that has happened," Catherine replied.

"Maybe we should go to check on her," Asbel said.

"She's fine. I told one of the guards to take care of her." Catherine said.

Meanwhile in the kitchen, the waitress yelled out Catherine, Rose and Marie's order.

"Do we have any more ribs?" Clover asked.

"I don't think so," the Sue chef replied.

"Are you serious!?" Clover exclaimed. She went to the freezer to check. She opened the door and started looking around. "Oh, thank god," she said as she spotted the ribs Marie had placed there. "Hey these are new, did we get a new shipment of ribs?" Clover yelled out the door,

"Not that I know of!"

"Weird." Clover said before shrugging and walking out the door.

Asbel, Catherine and Marie were waiting for their food. "They sure are taking a while." Asbel said.

"Be patient." Catherine said.

The waitress soon came over with the caviar.

"Thank you." Catherine said as the waitress set down the caviar before walking away. Marie looked at the caviar. Just looking at it made her want to gag. Catherine and Asbel started to eat their appetizer. Marie pushed it aside. The others continued to eat. Soon later the waitress came over with the food. She placed the three plates of ribs on the table.

"Enjoy your food." The waitress said before walking away. Marie looked down at her plate. Catherine used a fork to slide the rib off the bone. Asbel did the same. Marie hesitantly picked up her fork and removed the meat off the bone. Catherine began to cut into the rib with her knife and fork. Marie had a piece of the rib on her fork. She waited a second before putting it in her mouth. It tasted like regular pork ribs but sort of different.

Catherine noticed Asbel seemed frozen in place. "Are you alright?" Catherine asked. Asbel was barely able to mutter anything out. Her eyes were full of fear. Catherine looked at Marie with confusion. They both turned to look at Asbel.

"These ribs..." Asbel muttered.

"What's wrong with the ribs? Is it too tender for your liking?" Marie asked

Asbel's eyes grew wide and she looked distraught. She put her hand over her mouth in disgust. You could hear her breath grow heavy. "These ribs. These are not animal ribs.. IT'S HUMAN." shouted Asbel as she stood up in fright.

People started to look over, confused. Catherine and Marie looked at each other again confused and frightened. Catherine gave Marie an angry look and looked back as Asbel.

"Are you sure? The chances of that happening are very slim." said Catherine in a sarcastic tone.

"Yes! I'm positive! Look, you can see on the outer bones, there's more of a hard bend. Pork has a smooth curve on the ribs!" Asbel replied quickly. Asbel took a step back. Her face was filled with disgust and you could see her body trembling.

Clover came out of the kitchen and into the dining room. "Is everything alright in here?"

Asbel stared at Clover for a moment and finally walked over and grabbed Clover's hand and walked over to the other side of the dining room. Catherine and Marie watched as worry grew on Clover's face as Asbel went on to tell Clover what she had discovered.

"That's impossible!" Clover said.

"No, I'm positive! I'm a nurse and I know these things," Asbel said with a shaky voice.

"Listen, I trust your judgment as a nurse but there's no way that that meat is human," Clover said.

Catherine and Marie walked over to Asbel, "Asbel let's just go," Catherine said as she paid Clover for the food and gave her a generous tip.

She grabbed Asbel's hand and left the restaurant. "Asbel. I understand what's been happening is scary, but there's no reason to make a scene," Catherine said.

“I swear to god that that meat was human. Why won’t you believe me?” Asbel pleaded.

Catherine sighed. “Let’s get back to our rooms.” She held Asbel’s hand and took her to her room. Marie followed them.

Catherine led Asbel to her room. “I just want to go home,” Asbel said.

“I know.” Catherine said. “We'll be on land soon and the police will be able to solve this ordeal.” Asbel sighed and went into her room and shut the door.

Catherine and Marie started to walk to their rooms. “I can’t believe this. Why did we do this? We didn't have to feed Rose to Asbel, what’s the point of it?” Marie said.

“Shut the hell up.” Catherine said in an exhausted voice. They entered their room. “We have to cut the rest of this body.” Catherine said as she went to the bathroom. She pulled her knife out of her purse and set it on the vanity next to the door to the bathroom.

“I don't understand.. Why Rose? I understand the others but,” Marie said before Catherine cut her off.

“STOP. TALKING.” Marie rolled her eyes. Catherine turned around. “You know what I'll do it in the morning. I'm too tired for this.” Catherine closed the door to the bathroom. “You know what. Isn’t there a bar on this ship?”

“I think so.” Marie replied.

“We should go,” Catherine said. “It’ll be fun!”

Marie looked at her funny. “Why would we do that?”

“Why not?” Catherine said. She grabbed her purse and led Marie out the door.

"You seem awfully cheery after killing your friend… and eating her." "Marie said.

Catherine changed the subject. "I'm awfully hungry.. I was looking forward to our meal, too bad Asbel ruined it for us."

"Do you even know where the bar is?" Marie asked.

"Well no, but it shouldn't be that hard to find." Catherine said. They wandered around for a while before finding the bar. "Finally! We've been wandering around for forever!" Catherine said.

They entered the bar. There were people everywhere. They sat down in the chairs by the door and where they would wait to be seated.

"Why are we here again?" Marie asked.

"This whole trip has been so boring we should at least have some fun," Catherine said.

A waitress came up to them. "Follow me to your seats." She said. They followed her as she sat them at the bar.

"This sure is a nice place," Catherine said as she looked around. Marie nodded. The bartender walked up to them behind the counter. He handed them their menus.

"Let me know when you are ready to order," he said. They both opened their menus.

"I'm in the mood for a steak, how about you?" Catherine asked.

"I'll get the steak too, I suppose." Marie replied.

"Would you like anything to drink?" Catherine said. "I was thinking about getting a Bloody Mary."

"No, I'm fine," Marie said. They both put their menus down. The bartender came over to them

"Are you two ready to order?"

Catherine nodded. "We will have two medium

well steaks and a Bloody Mary."

"Alright." The bartender said as he took their menus. Marie looked down at her feet. She was so confused by this whole situation. Why would Catherine do this?

After waiting for a bit the bartender came over with the drink and the steaks.

"Thank you," Catherine said. She took a sip of her drink.

"I don't understand," Marie said. "Why did you do all this? Rose didn't deserve to die." Catherine didn't answer. "What is your plan? Are we going back to England?" Marie asked.

"No." Catherine replied.

"What!?" Marie exclaimed. "What about the house? Where are we going to live?"

"I sold the house when we left and bought a house in Portugal."

Marie was shocked. "Why? I don't understand."

"I couldn't stay there anymore Marie," Catherine said.

"You could've just left the others. Why kill them?" Marie asked. Catherine didn't answer. "Why leave in the first place? Why couldn't we stay?" Marie asked.

"I hated it there... even after everything that happened.. I couldn't stay there." Catherine said.

"But he's dead. You killed your husband, it's over, why wouldn't you be happy," Marie said.

"That house was a prison for me Marie. I couldn't stay there even though he's dead.." Catherine said.

"So you just pack up and leave? Without warning? And then you bring your friends down with you.." Marie said. "I thought you liked Rose."

Catherine took a sip of her drink. "I did." She said.

Meanwhile, Asbel was in her room. She had lost her necklace and was looking for it. "Where the hell is it!?" She exclaimed as she was pulling apart her bed. "It has to be here somewhere.. Or maybe I lost it at the restaurant." She went to the bathroom to see if it was in there. She opened all the cabinets and looked on the counter. Then she left her room and made her way to Catherine's.

She knocked but nobody answered. "Weird," she said. She tried opening the door to find out that it was unlocked. She entered the room. "Hello?" Nobody was there. She saw the knife on the vanity. She picked it up and realized it was covered in blood. "What the hell," she said.

She saw that the bathroom door was opened. She walked in and screamed as she saw Rose's dismembered body. She turned around and started to run only to bump into Catherine who was standing right in front of her. Asbel raised her knife and tried to stab her only for Catherine to grab her wrist and twist it.

"OW GODDAMNIT." Asbel yelled.

Catherine pulled a knife out of her pocket. Why does she have two!? Asbel thought. Catherine attempted to strike her but Asbel stopped her grabbing her wrists. She thrusted her arms to the side and attempted to stab her stomach. Catherine stopped her and tried to pry the knife out of her hands. She kicked her in the stomach causing her to let go of the knife. She took one of her knives and stabbed Asbel in the stomach. She fell back onto the floor.

Marie walked in. "What the hell!"

Catherine walked out of the bathroom. Marie still stood there. Looking at the two dead bodies.

Catherine came back into the bathroom with her bag. “I'm going to get ready for bed.” She said before closing the door on Marie. Marie grabbed her bag and changed in the room. Catherine came out of the bathroom to see that Marie was already asleep. She looked at her for a moment before going to bed herself.

The next morning. Marie woke up to the sound of Catherine putting Asbel and Rose’s body parts into bags. Marie sat up.

“It’s too early for this,” she complained. Catherine was humming a tune as she tied up the bags. “God, those smell horrible.” Marie said.

Catherine opened the window and threw them out.

“What..” Marie said before laying back down.

“Finally that's out of the way! The captain said we should be reaching our destination today!” Marie didn’t say anything because she was too tired. “Get ready! We have a big day ahead of us.” Catherine said.

Marie got out of bed and grabbed her maid attire and went to the bathroom. Catherine was already ready. Marie came out of the bathroom.

“We are going to get breakfast and then in a few hours we will be on land.” Catherine said. She grabbed her purse and Marie followed her out the door. They made their way to the restaurant.

They sat down at a table. Clover came over to them. “Oh hello! Clover, listen I would like to apologize for last night. Asbel’s been a bit shook up with all the deaths that have been happening,” Catherine said.

"Oh, it's alright I don't blame her it is really scary," Clover said. "Anyways, what would you two like to eat?"

"Can we get two cups of coffee please?" Catherine said.

Clover nodded. "We will bring that around shortly." She walked off.

"So what are we doing today?" Marie asked.

"Getting rid of the evidence," Catherine said.

"That's vague." Marie said. Clover brought over the coffee and set it down on the table.

"Thank you," Catherine said. They drank their coffee. Catherine placed her money and the table and they left.

"You still haven't told me our plan." Marie said.

Catherine grabbed her hand. "We need to go pack up!" She led her back to the room. She opened the door. Both of them started packing their things. Catherine gathered all of her makeup and clothes and put them in her bag. Marie packed up her nightgown. Catherine made the beds and cleaned up the bathroom. Soon enough they were all packed up. "In about thirty minutes the ship will be docked and we will be headed to the fuel bunker. "

"What!?" Marie exclaimed. Catherine didn't explain. Thirty minutes passed.

"Let's go," Catherine said. Catherine and Marie picked up their bags and headed to the boiler room. They ran all the way there. They finally made it. Catherine opened her purse and pulled out some matches.

"What is going on, what are you doing!?" Marie asked. Catherine didn't answer. She stood near the fuel tank. She lit the match. She opened the hatch to the fuel tank.

"I am going to throw this match down here, once I do we need to run." Catherine said.

"WHAT!?" Marie yelled.

Catherine threw the match. She grabbed Marie's hand and they ran out of there. The ship started bursting into flames behind them as they ran. They ran to the deck as fast as they could. They were shoving people as they ran onto shore. Their feet hit the ground. Suddenly.

The ship exploded. The impact pushed Catherine and Marie back a bit.

"WHAT THE HELL!?" Marie yelled. She was stunned. Everyone was screaming. Some made it onto the shore but others got caught in the explosion.

Clover had left the boat to pick up a shipment that came in late. She was carrying her crates of meat and vegetables. She was walking along the shore. When she looked up. She saw the ship. She stood there. Stunned looking at the boat with the crates of food. "Oh, no. I left my favorite spatula in there."

"What the hell.." Marie said again. She was very confused. She and Catherine stood near the shore. As people ran around them screaming.

Catherine looked at the water. "We should get going. I booked us a hotel, we will go see the new house tomorrow."

She started walking away from the shore. Marie followed after her. They walked away from the chaos.

The End

ABOUT THE AUTHORS

All of the authors are members of the Azalea Middle School Writer's Block. It is an after school club where students are given the support and time to write and pursue their passion for writing. The ladies spent a tremendous about of time and effort into their stories.

Made in the USA
Middletown, DE
13 August 2023

36660388R00056